xF   c.3
Koontz.
    Chicago and the cat.

                                    $12.99

DATE DUE		
SEP 22 1995		
MAN OCT 22 1995		
MN APR 30 1996		

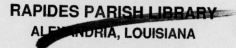
GAYLORD

CHICAGO AND THE CAT

The Halloween Party

WRITTEN AND ILLUSTRATED BY

Robin Michal Koontz

A LITTLE CHAPTER BOOK

COBBLEHILL BOOKS · DUTTON/NEW YORK

THIS BOOK IS FOR PEGGY,
who knows both ends of a horse better than anyone.

Library of Congress Cataloging-in-Publication Data
Koontz, Robin Michal.
Chicago and the cat : the Halloween party /
written and illustrated by Robin Michal Koontz.
p.   cm.
"A Little chapter book."
Summary: Despite careful planning and practice wearing their
joint costume, Chicago the rabbit and her friend the cat have
some surprises in store when they go to a Halloween party.
ISBN 0-525-65138-1
[1. Halloween—Fiction.   2. Costume—Fiction.   3. Rabbits—Fiction.
4. Cats—Fiction.]   I. Title.   II. Title: Halloween party.
PZ7.K83574Ch   1994   [E]—dc20   93-27043   CIP   AC

Published in the United States by Cobblehill Books,
an affiliate of Dutton Children's Books,
a division of Penguin Books USA Inc.,
375 Hudson Street, New York, New York 10014
Typography by Kathleen Westray
Printed in Hong Kong   First Edition
10   9   8   7   6   5   4   3   2   1

CHAPTER ONE

"Hey, cat!" yelled Chicago.

"Let's try on our

Halloween costume."

"What do you mean

'our' costume?" asked the cat.

"Check it out," said Chicago.

"We're going to be a horse!"

She held up the costume.

"No way," said the cat.

"I'm not wearing that silly thing."

"But there's a Halloween party
tomorrow night," said Chicago.
"A food party?" asked the cat.
"You bet," said Chicago.
The cat leaped from her chair.
"Let's try on that horse costume!"
she said.

"I'll wear the front part," said Chicago,

"and you wear the back part."

"No way," said the cat.

"Make it the other way around."

"Okay," said Chicago.

"You wear the back part, and
   I'll wear the front part."
"That's more like it," said the cat.
   They got into the horse costume.
"Is this what we decided?"
   she asked.

"Your part connects

to mine like this," said Chicago.

She zipped up the costume.

"Hey!" yelled the cat.

"Let's walk," said Chicago.

"One, two, three, look out!"

"I can't!" cried the cat.

"It's dark in here!"

Chicago and the cat

tumbled to the floor.

"I guess we need to practice,"
said Chicago.
"I guess so," grumbled the cat.

CHAPTER TWO

"I think we're getting

the hang of this," said Chicago.

"Now that I can see," said the cat.

Chicago and the cat clopped outside.

"Look, there's Mr. Walturs,"

whispered Chicago.

"Let's see if he knows us."

"Hello there, Horse," said Mr. Walturs.

"Would you like a carrot

from Chicago's garden?"

"Hey, it's us!" said Chicago.

"You fooled me," chuckled Mr. Walturs.

"What are you going to be
    at the party?" asked Chicago.
"A monster," said Mr. Walturs.
"I want to win
    the costume contest."
"Sounds great," said Chicago.
"See you tomorrow!"
    Chicago and the cat
    clopped back inside.

"You didn't tell me about
a costume contest," said the cat.
"Do you think we'll win?"
"Who cares?" said Chicago.
"We'll be a big hit, you'll see!"

CHAPTER THREE

"Hurry up!" yelled Chicago.

"It's time to

go to the party!"

"*Growwwlllll!*" screamed the cat.

She raced into the room.

"What have you done?"

cried Chicago.

"I'm a monster, like Mr. Walturs,"

replied the cat.

"But what about our

horse costume?" Chicago asked.

"Forget about it," said the cat.

"I want to win the

costume contest."

"Fine," said Chicago.

"We'll just see about that."

She stomped out the door.

The cat followed her.

"*Growwlllll!*" she cried.

Chicago and the cat
headed for the party.
"Whooo! Whooo! WHOOOOOOOO!"
"What was that?" cried the cat.
Two yellow eyes
gleamed in the darkness.

"I think it's a ghost," said Chicago.

A shadowy shape dived toward the cat.

"*Akkkkkkkkk!*" cried the cat.

She ran under a bush.

"Why is it after me?"

"Maybe ghosts don't like monsters,"

said Chicago.

"But I'm not a monster!"

screamed the cat.

She jumped into the back

of the horse costume and zipped it shut.

"Let's get out of here!" she cried.

"Whatever you say," said Chicago.

CHAPTER FOUR

"Look at those kids," said Chicago.

"Their bags are full of treats!"

"Let's go trick or treating!"
   said the cat.

"But what about the party?"
asked Chicago.
"We might miss the costume contest!"
"No we won't," said the cat.
"Come on, let's get some candy."
"Oh, all right," said Chicago.
They clopped up to a house.
Chicago kicked at the door.

The door creaked open.

Chicago peeked in the doorway.

"It's dark in there," she said.

Just then a huge yellow grin appeared.

"*Owwooooooooooooooo!*" cried the grin.

"RUN!" yelled Chicago.

"Wait for me!" yelled the cat.

She bumped after Chicago.

They ran into the woods.

"Do you think it

chased us?" asked Chicago.

The cat peered out from behind Chicago.

"I think it went the other way," she said.

"Thank goodness," said Chicago.

"Let's go to the party."

CHAPTER FIVE

"Where have you two been?"
asked Mr. Walturs.
"We had the costume contest
without you!"

"Who won?" asked the cat.

"Barney," said Mr. Walturs.

"Isn't that a clever costume?"

The huge yellow grin appeared.

"*Owwoooooooooooooo!*" cried Barney.

"Very clever," said the cat.

She looked around.

"Hey, where's the food?"

"Oh, dear," said Mr. Walturs.

"The refreshments are all gone."

"What?" cried the cat.

"Don't be rude," said Chicago.

"We have plenty to eat at home."

"Then let's go home," said the cat.

"Great idea," said Chicago.

"Come on everybody,

 let's go to our house!"

"That's not what

 I meant," grumbled the cat.

"Come on," said Chicago.

"We'll have fun."

They all headed for their house.

"Let's eat!" said the cat.

"Let's bob for apples!" said Mr. Walturs.

"Let's play pin the tail

on the donkey!" said Barney.

"That was a fun party," said Chicago.

"And we were a big hit
  in our horse costume."

"Except when it was Barney's turn
  to pin the tail on the donkey,"
  said the cat.

"That was not fun."

"Barney said he was sorry," said Chicago.

"Right," said the cat.

"Next year you get to wear the back part."

"No way," said Chicago, "I'm planning
a different costume for next year!"

"Oh, no, what is it?" asked the cat.

"We'll talk about that later," said Chicago.

"Happy Halloween!"